Sit! Stay! Read!

MY DOG TOBY

Andrea Zimmerman

Andrea Zimmerman and David Clemesha

ILLUSTRATED BY True Kelley

SILVER WHISTLE · HARCOURT, INC.

SAN DIEGO   NEW YORK   LONDON

Library of Congress Cataloging-in-Publication Data
Zimmerman, Andrea Griffing.
My dog Toby/Andrea Zimmerman and David Clemesha; illustrated by True Kelley.
p.   cm.
"Silver Whistle."
Summary: Toby the dog is a beloved pet, but he doesn't seem to be able to do any tricks.
ISBN 0-15-202014-4
[1. Dogs—Fiction.]   I. Clemesha, David.   II. Kelley, True, ill.   III. Title.
PZ7.Z618My   2000
[E]—dc21   98-35246

F E D C

Printed in Hong Kong

The illustrations in this book were done in Luma Dyes watercolors, acrylics,
and pen and ink on Fabriano watercolor paper.
The display type was set in Boink.
The text type was set in Pike.
Color separations by Bright Arts Ltd., Hong Kong
Printed by South China Printing Company, Ltd., Hong Kong
This book was printed on totally chlorine-free Nymolla Matte Art paper.
Production supervision by Stanley Redfern and Ginger Boyer
Designed by Kaelin Chappell and True Kelley

To Jane, Steve, Alex, and Jordan—animal lovers

—A. Z. and D. C.

To Chewy Ann Pesky, Moby Dick Udaman, Yo Boy,
Jane Panache, Divine Miss Whoopi, Charles,
Bo Bo the Magnificent Wannabe Circus Dog,
and Marth

—T. K.

My dog is white and brown.
He has short legs and long ears.
He likes to smell things.

And scratch.

His name is Toby.

When I get home from school,
Toby is watching for me through the front window.

And when I open the door,
he wags his tail and
licks my legs.

He's so happy when I feed him.
I can tell by the way he looks at me.

We like to pull on an old sock.
It's Toby's favorite game.

When we go outside, he chases me all around.

At night, Toby sleeps by my side.

He barks to protect me.

But my dog Toby has never done a trick. I tried "Sit."

I tried "Roll over."

Beg ?

I tried "Beg."

I tried "Fetch."

Fetch!

...dumb dog...

Toby didn't do any of these things.
My brother says maybe he's dumb.
Toby's not dumb.
My brother's dumb.

My friend Philip's dog can shake hands.

Michael's dog can play soccer.

Melanie's dog can bring in the newspaper.

Kristie's dog can dance.

My dog Toby can't do any of these things.

Maybe Toby doesn't speak English.

My friend Juan tried
"Sit" in Spanish.

I asked Mr. Wong next door
to try Chinese.

Pierre tried French.

Maya tried Japanese.

I don't think Toby speaks
another language.

He just speaks Dog.

My brother still says maybe he's dumb.
Toby's not dumb.
My brother's dumb.

Toby is smart.
He knows where the gopher is
digging in the yard.

He knows if you drop a piece of sandwich in his food dish,

even if he's
way upstairs.

He knows when it's five o'clock and time to go for a walk.

He probably even knows
my brother is dumb.

But I wish Toby
could do a trick.

I thought maybe I could learn to speak Dog.
I tried, but I didn't know what I was saying.

WOOF AWOOOoo ARK ARK GRRFF RUFF!

Neither did Toby.

Then I thought maybe Toby could learn to speak English.
It's not so hard. Even my brother can do it.

"Sit!" I said. I showed him how.

"Sit!" I said in
the morning.

"Sit!" I said after school.

"Sit!" I said at the park.
"SIT!"

We practiced all the time.

Then one morning I looked deep into Toby's eyes.
He looked deep into my eyes.
We looked for a long time.

"Sit," I said.

Slowly, slowly, his back end lowered.

Toby sat!

He did it!
Toby learned a trick!

I hugged him and he barked and we ran around.

"Watch this," I told my brother.
"Sit!"
Toby sat.

"Wow!" yelled my brother.
"He's a smart dog!"

He sure is.

And I love him so.

Maybe someday he'll even learn another trick.

But I don't care if he never learns to shake or beg or roll over.

I'll always love Toby.

And I guess my brother's not so dumb after all.